Y0-CBC-032

Dear Maddy and Wendy,
Dairy Farmers Rule!
♡ Sue

Helper Cow

Fresh Cream Dreams!
Anne

Sue MacVeety

Illustrated by Anne Douglas

Pentland Press, Inc.
www.pentlandpressusa.com

PUBLISHED BY PENTLAND PRESS, INC.
5122 Bur Oak Circle, Raleigh, North Carolina 27612
United States of America
919-782-0281

ISBN 1-57197-307-9
Library of Congress Control Number: 2001 135255

Copyright © 2001 Sue MacVeety

All rights reserved, which includes the right to
reproduce this book or portions thereof in any form
whatsoever except as provided by the U.S. Copyright Law.

Printed in China

To Grandma Josie and Papa Arn
for enabling us to live a homestead lifestyle.

Helper Cow by Bob MacVeety

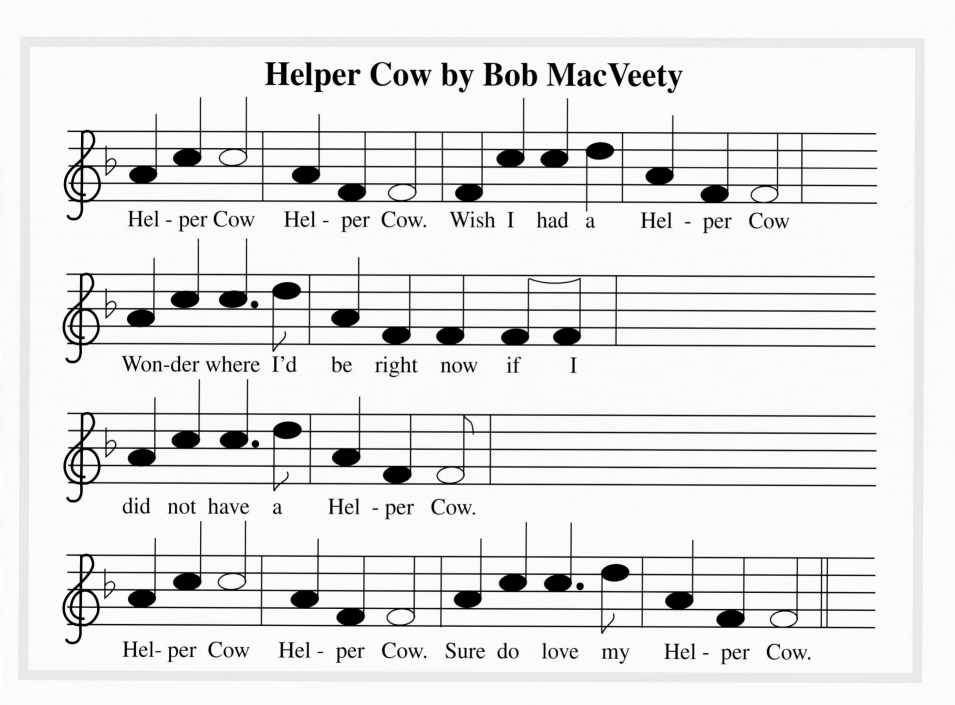

Jazz is a big, beautiful, brown-eyed, two-horned, fawn-colored Jersey cow. Her real name is Jasmine. She is sweet and gentle as a cow can be.

She eats clover and tender green grass shoots growing in the pasture. She lies in the sun for hours chewing her cud and contemplating life from a cow's eye view.

Jasmine can sit on her haunches just like a dog. She will sniff the breezes as she basks in bovine glory. This is Jazz, but at times she turns into HELPER COW.

Helper Cow hears the farm husband and wife drive the tractor to the woodlot to cut firewood. Helper Cow stands right where the tree is going to fall. All work must stop so she can be patted and pulled and cajoled and distracted to move out of the way so she's not squished.

Then Jazz hangs her head over the chopping block where the farmer tries to split his firewood. All work must stop so she can be patted and pulled and cajoled and distracted to move out of the way so she's not squashed. The farmer smiles and sings "Helper Cow."

Helper cow, helper cow, wish I had a helper cow.
Wonder where I'd be right now if I did not have a helper cow.
Helper cow, helper cow, sure do love my helper cow.

9

When the farmers need to muck out the bottom of the barn, Helper Cow stands right where they need to rake and shovel. All work must stop so she can be patted and pulled and cajoled and distracted to move out of the way so she's not hurt. And the farmers grin and sing "Helper Cow."

Helper cow, helper cow, wish I had a helper cow.
Wonder where I'd be right now if I did not have a helper cow.
Helper cow, helper cow, sure do love my helper cow.

When the farmers have been cutting brush all day to clear the pasture and they load it on the wagon to haul away, Helper Cow takes branches in her mouth and pulls them off the wagon. All work must stop so she can be patted and pulled and cajoled and distracted to move out of the way so she's not scratched. The farmers grin and sing "Helper Cow."

Helper cow, helper cow, wish I had a helper cow.
Wonder where I'd be right now if I did not have a helper cow.
Helper cow, helper cow, sure do love my helper cow.

Now the farm husband and wife plant peas and watch them come up sweet and tender. The day before they're ready to be picked, Helper Cow walks through the fence to eat all the peas. All work must stop so she can be patted and pulled and cajoled and distracted to move out of the way so she's not turned into hamburger. The farmers grin and sing "Helper Cow."

Helper cow, helper cow, wish I had a helper cow.
Wonder where I'd be right now if I did not have a helper cow.
Helper cow, helper cow, sure do love my helper cow.

When the farmers are loading fresh mown hay into the barn, Helper Cow climbs the stairs to eat the hay. All work must stop so she can be patted and pulled and cajoled and distracted to move out of the way so she doesn't get a stomach ache. The farmers smirk and sing "Helper Cow."

Helper cow, helper cow, wish I had a helper cow.
Wonder where I'd be right now if I did not have a helper cow.
Helper cow, helper cow, sure do love my helper cow.

When the farmers have worked a very long day, they decide to sit a spell on the porch to watch the sunset. A car pulls into the driveway. People jump out to say, "There's a big, beautiful, brown-eyed, two-horned cow walking the roads. Do you know her?" Everything but cow worship must stop so she can be patted and pulled and cajoled and distracted to move out of the way so she's not run over. The farmers laugh out loud and sing "Helper Cow."

Helper cow, helper cow, wish I had a helper cow.
Wonder where I'd be right now if I did not have a helper cow.
Helper cow, helper cow, sure do love my helper cow.

How to Make Butter from Jersey Milk

Tie the cow very tightly near a big pan of molasses grain. Wash her udder with warm, soapy water. Get a stream of milk out of each quarter. Dispose of this milk, as it may contain bacteria. Then milk into a stainless steel bucket. Be sure the cow does not step into the bucket and spill all the milk or contaminate it. Also, be sure she does not hit you in the head with her tail. Finish milking and let the cow loose into the pasture.

Bring the bucket inside. Pour the milk through a milk strainer into big enamel pans. (The strainer removes unwanted hair and such.) Put the milk pan in a cool place or in a refrigerator. Let the milk sit overnight. In the morning skim the thick, yellow cream off the top with the cream skimmer. Put the cream in a glass butter churn with wooden paddles. Let it sit at room temperature. Churn the butter. Keep turning and turning until it clumps and sits in buttermilk. Pour the buttermilk into a glass. Take the lump of butter and put it into a colander. Run cold water over it and squeeze until all the buttermilk is out. Put the butter into a hand-carved butter-mold. Refrigerate the butter. Use the buttermilk to make biscuits or pancakes. Eat. YUM!

The End

About the Author

Sue MacVeety received her bachelor's degree in Elementary Education from Boston University and her master's degree in Special Education from Lesley College. She has taught preschool through kindergarten since the 1970s and has been an adjunct faculty member at Berkshire Community College for the last fifteen years. She is a member of the National Association for Education for Young Children, the Audubon Society, and the Nature Conservancy.

Sue is an avid gardener, herbalist, horseback rider, swimmer, and hiker. She also loves to work on her farm where she raises chickens, horses, cats, dogs and, of course, cows. Jasmine, the Helper Cow, was born on her family's farm. Sue's husband, Bob, would sing the "Helper Cow" song to Jasmine while he worked on the farm. Sue MacVeety has been married to Bob for twenty-eight years and is the mother of two grown children.

Below is a photograph of Jasmine and the author's daughter, Jessica, who hand-raised the Helper Cow.